2024 written by Nadine Holland and Illustrated by Miss Khan
Nadine Holland & Miss Khan are part of HB Publishing House.
All rights reserved. No part of this publication may be
reproduced, stored in a retrieval system, or transmitted, in any
form or in any means - by electronic, mechanical, photocopying,
recording or otherwise - without prior written permission.
Kiko and the Coralline Crest
HB Publishing House, 21, NG13 7AW
British Library Catalogue in Publication Data: a catalogue
record for this book is available from the British Library.
ISBN: 9781068642715

For my Mum, Sheila, who inspired this book.

KIKO
and the coralline crest

Written by Nadine Holland   Illustrated by Miss Khan

Below the warm waves,
not so far from the shore,

where bright sunlight dances
across the sea floor.

A small figure trembled alone and afraid.

Wrapped safe in some seaweed,
she hid in the shade.

Kiko the seahorse looked out to the west,

and sighed as she spotted
the Coralline Crest.

The reef glittered softly, the fish were so grand.
Elegant shells lined the glistening sand.

All of her life she'd had only one wish.
To swim to the Crest to admire all the fish.

And once, long ago, little Kiko had tried.

But she was so small
and the bay was so wide,

that Kiko got caught,

in the pull of the tide.

She crashed through the waves and was left...

...terrified.

When Kiko now gazes across the wide bay,

she only
remembers that
terrible day.

The panic starts rising, her chest feels too tight,

so Kiko slips back to the shade,

out of sight.

Then one day, the waves seemed to ripple and

THRUM.

And Kiko looked out for the source of the hum.

The reef was alive with magnificent schools,

each fish was unique,

how they shimmered like jewels.

"That does it!" said Kiko,
"today is the day,
I don't want to miss this, I

WILL

cross the bay!"

So, quivering, Kiko peeped out from her leaf,

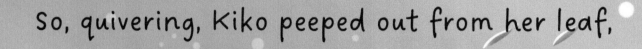

and saw a pink shell on the path to the reef.

She took a deep breath,
set her sights on the shell.

Then darted out quickly...
right into a swell.

Tumbling and churning,
the seahorse was thrown,

back into the weeds with
a pitiful groan.

But Kiko, determined, went
back to her plan.
"I must reach the Crest
any way that I can."

The second time,
    reaching the pink shell was easy,

and Kiko was feeling less anxious
                    and queasy.

            She spotted a net
        on the seabed ahead,

                took a deep breath,
                and then onwards
                she sped.

Focusing hard on the net - her next goal,
poor Kiko did not see the Triggerfish shoal.

They slammed her,
and swooshed her,
and knocked her off course.

So back to the
weeds

went the little seahorse.

A turtle swam near as poor Kiko was shaking, her stomach was stirring, her body was aching.

She sobbed as her heart pounded hard in her chest,

but Kiko was set upon reaching the Crest.

"I know I can do this!" she cried, breathing fast,

and clutched at a fin
as the turtle slipped past.

They cruised past the shell
and the net on their way,

and Kiko thought,
"Goodness I've
crossed the whole
bay!"

But just as they started their ultimate glide.

A spine-chilling shadow washed in with the tide.

The shadow turned into a

HUGE

manta ray!

And all of the beautiful fish...

...swam

...away.

Kiko snuck into a crevice to hide.

And filled with frustration she cried and she cried.

"I travelled so far, I was practically there! And now they're all gone, why is life so unfair?"

But after a while, Kiko had a new thought.
All of her struggles had not been for naught.

She'd faced all her
fears, gone so far
and so fast...

The dread

and the panic

had ended,

at last.

Now Kiko can go, anytime to the reef.
She no longer trembles behind her old leaf.

Her world opened up, from the east to the west.
On the day that she got to...

...The Coralline Crest.

Meet the author

Nadine grew up in Devon in the era of leg warmers, cassette tapes and scary public information adverts. The world baffled her a bit and so she preferred to bury her nose in books and one day dreamt of becoming a writer herself – mostly so that she would finally know enough words to beat her Grandad at Scrabble.

Kiko was written to give voice to the feelings we have when worry, fear and panic take over; sometimes because of scary experiences in the past, sometimes because of mental health disorders, and sometimes just because. But it is also a reminder that even though we can find things challenging we can still have big goals, and with the right plan we can find a way to achieve them.

Nadine loves to write picture books, chapter books, middle grade novels and poetry. She lives in Gloucestershire, surrounded by magical hills and ancient forests, where she lives with her husband, her daughter, three silly cats, and a dog with giant ears.

You can follow Nadine here:
X: @Writes_Nadine
Insta: @nadinehastowrite
TikTok: @writes_nadine
Threads: @nadinehastowrite

Let's be friends...

www.hbpublishinghouse.co.uk

hb_publishing_house

HB Publishing House

hb_publishing_house

Milton Keynes UK
Ingram Content Group UK Ltd.
UKHW021345190624
444359UK00002B/55